What shall I be?

Ray Gibson

Designed by Amanda Barlow

Edited by Fiona Watt

Illustrated by Mikki Rain

Photographs by Ray Moller

and Howard Allman

Face painting by Caro Childs

Series Editor: Jenny Tyler

Contents

With thanks to Ben Bokaie, Raz Budeiri, Inigo Choong, Kezia Evans, Pippa Green, Jessica Hopf, James Jacob, Martha Kiff, Kattja Madrell, Emma Pearson, William Rowlands, Kyrie Simon-Penfold and Yasmin Wilson

A circus strongman

Print or paint shapes on material (see right).

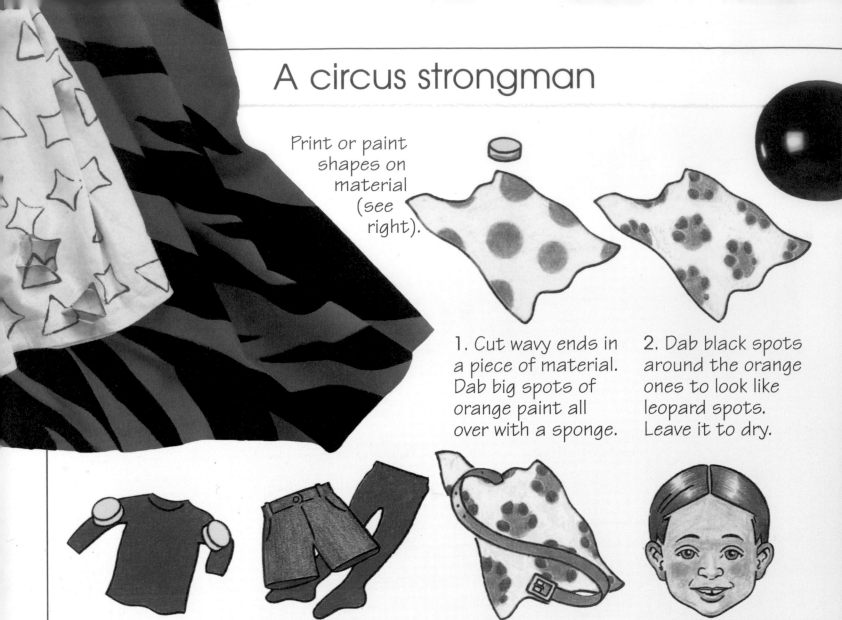

1. Cut wavy ends in a piece of material. Dab big spots of orange paint all over with a sponge.

2. Dab black spots around the orange ones to look like leopard spots. Leave it to dry.

3. Tape a sponge to the top of each of your arms. Pull on a long-sleeved T-shirt over the top.

4. Pull on a pair of bright tights then put on a pair of dark shorts on top of them.

5. Put the spotty material over one shoulder. Fasten it around your waist with a belt.

6. Put some hair gel in your hair. Part your hair in the middle and smooth it down.

Make some weights

7. Dip a damp sponge in red face paint. Dab it lightly over your cheeks.

8. Use a brush and dark face paint to to draw big eyebrows. Add a curly moustache.

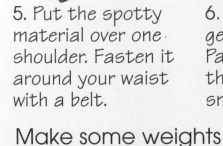

1. Blow up two balloons. Paint two tubes from the middle of kitchen paper towels.

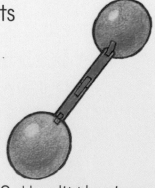

2. Use little pieces of tape to join the tubes together. Tape a balloon on at each end.

Print shapes on a
bright vest with
paint and a
cookie cutter.

Face paint a
hairy chest.

A scarecrow

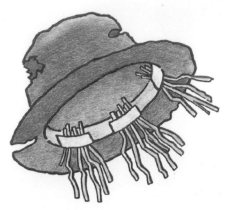

1. Tape lots of clean dry straw or long grass inside an old hat.

2. Sponge brown face paint in patches on your face. Sponge red on your cheeks.

3. Brush on spikey eyebrows and a moustache with brown face paint.

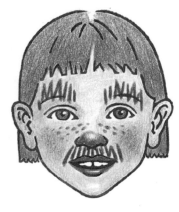

4. Dab face paint on your nose and add big freckles. Brush red on your lips too.

5. Pull on a big checked shirt and some old trousers or a skirt.

6. Put on some old boots or shoes. Put elastic bands around your ankles.

7. Put elastic bands around your wrists. Don't make them tight.

8. Push straw into your cuffs and trouser legs, under the elastic bands.

Tie a bright scarf around your neck and pin a toy mouse to your hat.

Put a belt around your tummy and push straw under it.

A snow queen

Make a crown

  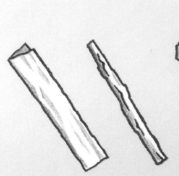 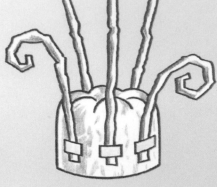

I. Spread glue inside the bottom part of a big plastic bottle. Press pieces of foil onto it.

2. Cut out four pieces of foil as big as this book. Cut each piece in two from end to end.

3. Fold each piece of foil in half like this. Squeeze each one into a long, thin shape.

4. Tape five of the pieces evenly around the bottom of the crown. Curl the ends over.

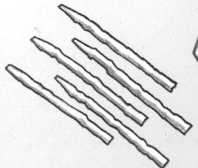 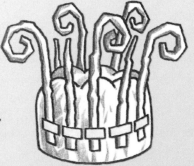  

5. Cut the other pieces of foil in half. Pinch one end to make pointed icicles.

6. Tape five of the icicles around the bottle in between the long ones. There will be one icicle left.

7. Cut some foil as long as this book. Fold it over and over. Tape it around the bottom of the crown.

8. Wrap the spare icicle around one of your fingers for a ring. Twist the end into a spiral shape.

Snowflakes

1. Cut a small square of thin white or silver paper.

2. Fold the square diagonally to make a triangle. Fold it in half again.

3. Cut different shapes along each edge then open it out and flatten it.

A wand

Cover a thin garden cane in foil. Glue a snowflake to one end of it.

See pages 30-31 to paint your face like this.

Press some self-adhesive stars onto your hair.

Use an old skirt or piece of material for a cloak. Glue or pin on some snowflakes and stars.

Attach the crown to your hair with hairgrips.

Fasten the cloak with a brooch.

A puppy

1. If your hair is short, tie a ribbon or a piece of elastic around your head.

2. Stuff a pair of short socks with lots of cotton wool balls.

1. If your hair is long, tie it into two high bunches.

3. Tuck the socks into the band. Use hairgrips to hold them in place.

4. Dab white face paint over your face. Close your eyes when you get near them.

2. Push each bunch into a short sock. Fasten them with bands.

5. Dab orange face paint on in patches. Brush black on the end of your nose.

6. Use a brush and brown face paint to add spots and big patches.

7. Brush a black line from your nose to your top lip. Brush along your lip too.

8. Add a red tongue on your bottom lip. Add dots either side of your nose.

After you have painted your face, put socks on your hands and feet, for paws.

A lucky pirate

1. Sponge light brown face paint over your face.

2. Brush on big eyebrows and a curly moustache.

3. Dab stubble on your chin with a toothbrush.

4. Cut out an eyepatch shape from stiff black paper.

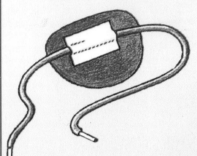   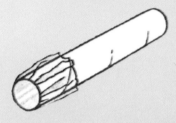

5. Tape a bootlace across the back of the eyepatch, near to the top.

6. Get someone to tie the eyepatch and knot a scarf around your head.

7. Slip an elastic band through a curtain ring. Hang it over your ear.

8. For a telescope, paint a cardboard tube. Put foodwrap over one end.

Use face paint to make a scar on your cheek.

Put some old necklaces and brooches in your treasure box too.

Make a treasure box

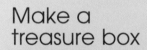

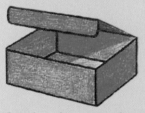

Find a box with a lid, like a chocolate or teabag box. Paint it.

Cover things like bottle tops and biscuits with foil to make treasure.

You could safety pin a toy parrot on your shoulder.

Face paint a curly beard instead of stubble.

Wear a leather belt across one shoulder.

A doctor

1. For a doctor's coat, use an old white shirt. Cut the sleeves to fit.

2. Push the lenses out of old sunglasses. Wear the frames.

3. For medicine, fill plastic bottles with water. Add a few drops of food dye.

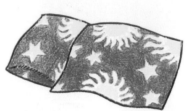

4. Use a pillow for a bed. Fold a pillowcase in half for a top sheet.

Make a stethoscope

1. Cut a piece of foil twice as long as this book. Fold it in half.

2. Fold the foil in half again then scrunch it up tightly.

3. Fold the foil in half. Pull the two ends apart and bend them in.

4. Cut a piece of foil as big as this book. Fold it and scrunch it up.

Use a lunch box for a doctor's case.

Make bandages from strips of material.

5. Bend one end around the long piece. Tape a jar lid on the other end.

Make a thermometer

Cut a strip of foil. Wrap it around the end of a straw and tape it on.

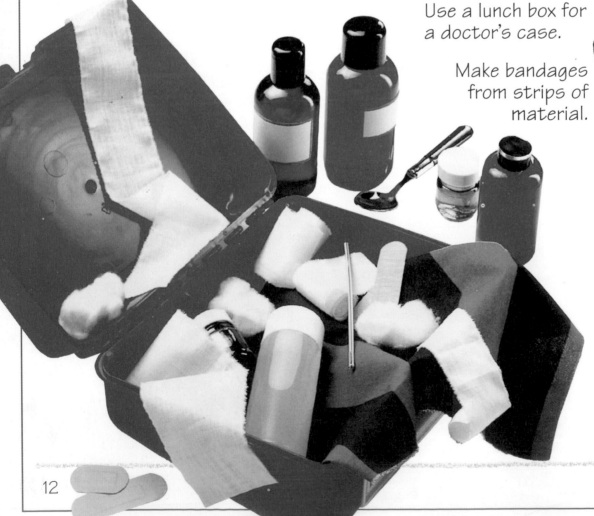

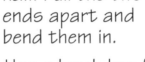

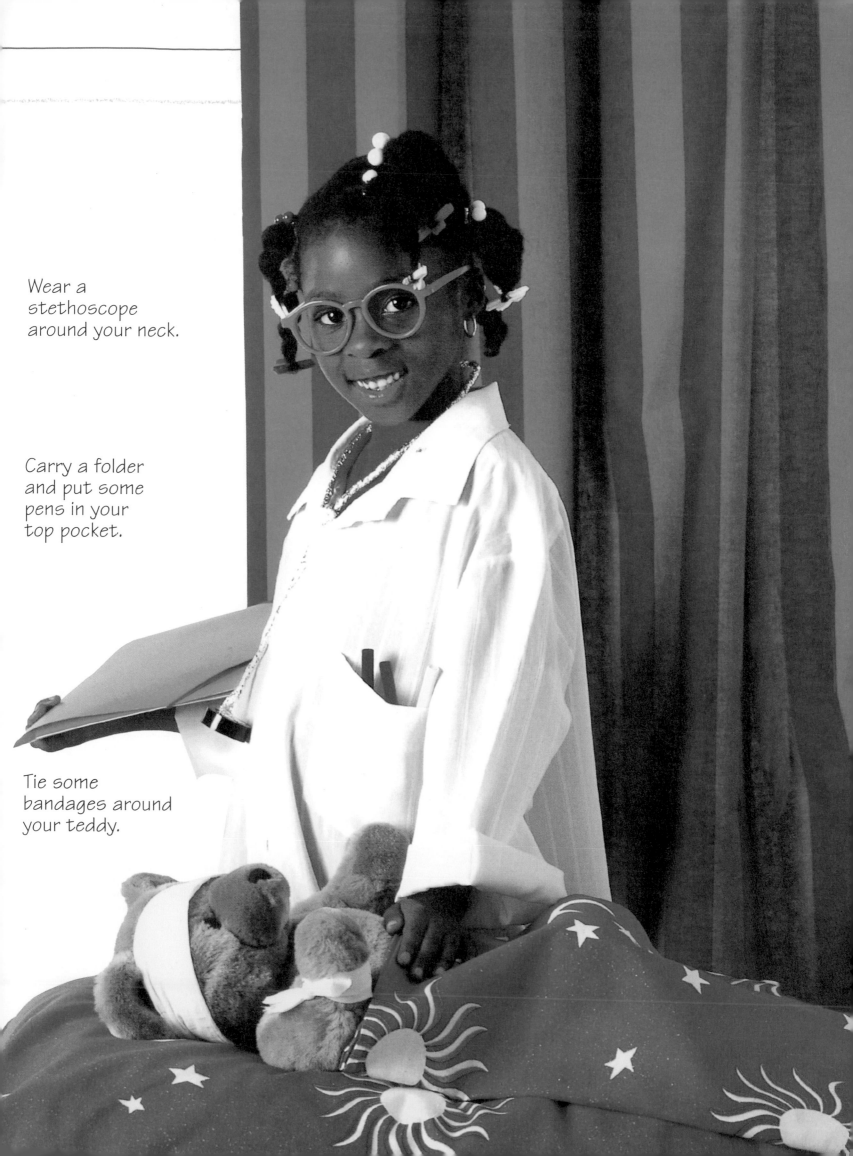

Wear a stethoscope around your neck.

Carry a folder and put some pens in your top pocket.

Tie some bandages around your teddy.

A spotted bug

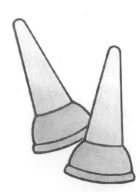

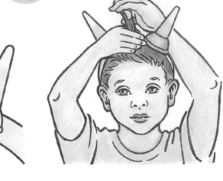

1. Put two ice-cream cones on newspaper. Paint them then leave them to dry.

2. Cut a strip of thin cardboard to fit over the top of your head. Glue the cones onto it.

3. Bend the cardboard around your head. Fasten it at each side with hairgrips.

4. Put a blob of hair gel onto your hand. Lift up a big clump of your hair in your other hand.

Remember you can't eat the cones once they are painted.

5. Squeeze your gelled hand around a clump of hair and pull it up. Do this to more clumps of hair.

6. Rub a damp sponge in face paint. Dab it over your face. Leave gaps for spots.

7. Use a brush and a different face paint to draw the outlines of spots in the gaps.

8. Fill in the spots with a brush. Close your eye when you fill in any spots that are near it.

Put face paint on your hands and arms.

Cut out spots and tape them onto a bright T-shirt.

A rich lady

Make some bank notes

1. Cut four pieces of newspaper as big as this book. Fold them in half like this.

2. Fold the top edge down to the bottom. Then fold the top down to the bottom again.

3. Open out each piece of paper. Cut carefully along all the lines you have folded.

4. Write numbers on each piece of paper with a felt-tip pen. Keep them in a handbag.

Carry lots of bright shiny things in a handbag.

5. Pull on a bright T-shirt and a long floaty skirt. Put a belt around your waist.

6. Put on bright lipstick. Dab some pink powder or face paint on your cheeks.

7. Put on several necklaces, brooches and some big earrings. Wear a watch.

Carry a toy dog. Tie a belt around its neck for a lead.

Put on some sunglasses.

Wear a long scarf around your shoulders for a shawl.

8. Wrap a ribbon around a big hat. Use a safety pin to attach some big flowers on the side.

9. Scrunch up some paper and push it into the toes of a pair of high-heeled shoes.

10. Put on the shoes and the hat. Put on some gloves and wear lots of rings on top of them.

Carry a handbag.

A funny clown

1. Sponge white all over your face. Draw red circles on your cheeks and nose.

2. Brush a big smiley shape around your mouth and fill it in.

3. Brush two arch shapes over your eyes and fill them in carefully.

4. Carefully draw black lines across your eyes. Add thin eyebrows.

Wear a bright T-shirt. Cut buttons from felt or paper and tape or glue them on.

Wear trousers that are too big for you. Use safety pins to attach ribbons, for braces.

Make a clown hat

1. Cut a roll of bright crêpe paper as wide as this book.

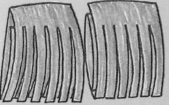

2. Cut the paper in two. Make cuts nearly to the top of each piece.

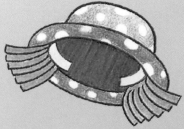

3. Tape the uncut edges inside a big hat. Tape them on at the sides.

4. Shake the hat to fluff out the hair. Tape on a fake flower at one side.

Big bow tie

1. Cut a piece of crêpe paper the same size as this book.

2. Fold it in half, long sides together. Put an elastic band around the middle.

3. Stretch out the two ends. Press on self-adhesive or gummed shapes.

4. Put a safety pin through the elastic band and fasten it onto your clothes.

A chef on television

Make a chef's hat

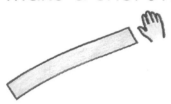

1. Cut a strip of white cardboard as tall as your hand and which fits around your head.

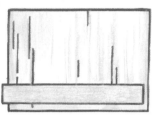

2. Cut a piece of white crêpe paper so it is the same length as the cardboard.

3. Lay the cardboard near the bottom of the paper. Fold the bottom edge over and tape it in place.

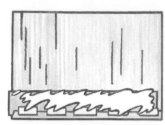

4. Put glue on the cardboard. Fold the cardboard over onto the crêpe paper and press it flat.

5. Hold the paper at each side. Pull your hands apart gently to stretch the paper like this.

6. Bend the cardboard around your head. Use small pieces of tape to join the ends.

7. Gather the top edge of the paper together and wrap an elastic band around it.

8. Press down the top of your hat so that it is flat on top. Puff it out around the sides.

Joke sausages

1. Carefully cut one leg from an old pair of pink or brown tights.

2. Squeeze four sheets of toilet paper to make a sausage shape.

3. Roll four pieces of paper around the sausage. Push it into the tights.

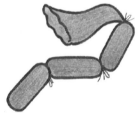

4. Tie thread at the end of the sausage. Make more sausages the same way.

Dressing up

Brush on a moustache with face paint. Add a little beard.

Put on an apron. Dip your fingers in flour and dab them over the apron.

Act as if you are doing a television show about cooking.

Dab some flour on your nose.

Collect some bowls, pans and spoons from your kitchen. Put them on a table in front of you.

Cinderella

Before

Pull some wispy bits from cotton wool and put it in your hair, as cobwebs.

1. Cut the bottom of an old skirt into rags. Sew or use safety pins to add bright patches.

2. Use a safety pin to fasten a piece of bright material around your waist as an apron.

3. Fold a scarf like this. Wrap it around your shoulders and knot the ends in front of you.

4. Sponge some pink face paint on your cheeks. Add some grey for dirty patches.

Make a broom

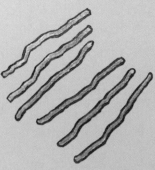

1. Collect lots of thin twigs. Snap them so that they are all about the same length.

2. Make them into a bunch around a garden cane. Wrap string around and around then tie it.

After

1. Pull on some pale tights and put on a pretty vest, leotard or swimsuit.

2. Tie some elastic around your waist. Tuck a piece of net curtain into it for a skirt.

3. Tie a strip of material or a piece of ribbon around your waist to hide the elastic.

4. For gloves, cut half way down the legs of some old lacy tights. Cut the toes off too.

Paint your face

1. Dip a paintbrush in red face paint. Brush red flowers on your forehead and on your cheeks.

2. Brush a bow near each eyebrow and wavy lines between the flowers. Add green leaves too.

Make a pretty fan (see page 25).

Tie bows on your shoulders and in your hair.

Glue fake flowers to your skirt.

Cinderella's sisters

Make a wig

1. Cut a piece of cotton wool roll as wide as this page. Then cut it into eight pieces.

2. Twist each piece to make ringlets. Clip them to your hair in front of your ears.

3. Cut another piece of cotton wool and clip it over your head to cover your hair.

4. Pull the cotton wool a little to make it lumpy. Glue on a big bright bow from a parcel.

Paint your face

1. Sponge pale pink face paint all over your face. Make your cheeks a darker pink.

For a bright wig, dab paint on the cotton wool and let it dry before you put it on.

2. Brush on long eyelashes. Put on some very bright lipstick and add a beauty spot.

Make a fan

1. Cut a piece of gift wrap so that it is as wide as this book and twice as long.

2. Fold over one of the short edges. Turn the gift wrap over then fold the edge up again.

3. Keep folding the gift wrap over and over in this way until you get to the end of it.

4. Wrap some tape around it at the bottom. Snip shapes out at the top. Open it out.

Instead of a wig, make two plaits from wool. Use hairgrips to clip them to your hair.

Tie a scarf around your head to hide the ends of the plaits.

Long nails

Cut ten pointy shapes from sticky paper. Lick them and press them over your own nails.

Put on some necklaces and rings.

A long-armed giant

1. Scrunch up paper and push it into a pair of rubber gloves to make them stiff.

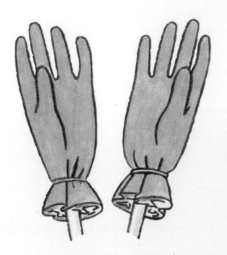

2. Push the round ends of two wooden spoons inside. Fix them with elastic bands.

3. Push a cushion up under your T-shirt to make a very fat tummy.

4. Put a big sweater over your T-shirt. Fasten a belt around your waist.

5. Dip a damp sponge in red face paint and dab it on your nose and cheeks.

6. Wet a brush and dip it into dark face paint. Draw on bushy eyebrows.

7. Face paint wiggly shapes across your chin to make a curly beard.

8. Add dark freckles across your nose and paint white teeth on your bottom lip.

9. Pull your cuffs over the ends of the gloves. Fasten them with elastic bands.

Wear big boots and a waistcoat.

Hold the handles of the spoons when you move your arms.

A very old person

1. Brush your hair back. Use a sponge to stroke grey or white face paint over your hair.

2. Dip the sponge in pale pink or white face paint and dab it all over your face.

3. Dab dark pink over your cheeks. Then dab some brown down each side of your nose.

4. Use a brush and brown face paint to add some thin lines across your forehead.

5. Brush two thin brown lines at the top of your nose, between your eyebrows.

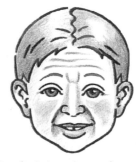

6. Add a line from each side of your nose to your mouth. Smudge the lines with your finger.

7. Dip a toothbrush in grey and dab it on your face for stubble, or put on bright lipstick.

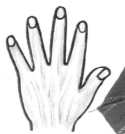

8. Brush thin blue or white lines on the back of your hands.

Collect some things like these to wear or carry.

For glasses, get someone to help you to take the lenses out of an old pair of sunglasses.

Wrap a scarf
around your neck
and wear a hat.

Painting your face

You can use face painting crayons, but the face paints which look like a box of paints are the best to use.

1. Make sure that your face is clean and dry. Put on the dressing-up clothes you are going to wear.

2. Wrap a towel around your neck to protect your clothes. Tie your hair back or put on a hairband.

3. To cover your face in face paint, dip a sponge in water then squeeze it until no more water comes out.

4. Rub the sponge around and around in the face paint. Dab it all over your face, right up to your hair.

5. Close each eye and dab over your eyelids very carefully. Press the sponge over your lips too.

Scarecrow
- page 4

Cinderella
- page 22

6. Wash your sponge and dip it into a different shade of face paint. Dab it lightly all over your cheeks.

7. Gently rub a thin wet paintbrush around in a face paint. Draw on eyebrows with the tip of the brush.

8. Use a thin paintbrush to add very fine lines on your forehead, around your eyes and on your cheeks.

  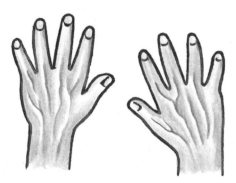

9. Use a paintbrush to add glitter face paint. Press little stars into it. They will stick as the paint dries.

10. Use face paint on your lips too. Brush around the shape of your lips then fill them in.

11. You can also put face paint on your hands and arms. Use a sponge to dab it on. Add lines with a brush.

Giant
- page 26

Clown
- page 18

Things you need

You will need face paints for most of the projects.

Strongman
yellow material
a belt
a long-sleeved T-shirt
two small sponges
a pair of shorts
hair gel
two balloons
two cardboard tubes
tape

Scarecrow
clean, dry straw or long
    grass
an old hat
old trousers or a skirt
checked shirt
old boots or shoes
elastic bands

Snow queen
3 litre plastic bottle
kitchen foil
white or silver paper
a thin garden cane

Puppy
a pair of short socks
cotton balls and a
    ribbon or some
    elastic (if your hair
    is short)
hairgrips
a ribbon
mittens

Pirate
stiff black paper
a bootlace
a bright scarf

Pirate: continued
a curtain ring
elastic band
a small box
things for treasure
a cardboard tube
plastic foodwrap

Doctor
an old white shirt
old sunglasses
plastic bottles
food dye
pillow and two pillowcases
kitchen foil
a jar lid
a straw

Spotted bug
two ice-cream cones
a strip of cardboard
paint
hairgrips
hair gel

Rich lady
a bright T-shirt
a long skirt
jewellery
a handbag
lipstick
face powder
newspaper

Funny clown
crêpe paper
big bright hat
self-adhesive or gummed
    shapes
a safety pin

A television chef
white cardboard
white crêpe paper
toilet paper
old brown or pink tights
thread
flour
striped apron

Cinderella
an old skirt
scraps of material
a big scarf
a brooch
thin twigs
a garden cane
pale tights
a vest, leotard or swimsuit
elastic and ribbon
a net curtain

Cinderella's sisters
cotton wool roll
hairgrips
bright parcel bow
gift wrap
sticky paper
old lacy tights

Long-armed giant
a pair of rubber gloves
two wooden spoons
a cushion
a belt
a big sweater
elastic bands

Very old person
old sunglasses
hat and scarf

This edition first published in 2003 by Usborne Publishing Ltd., Usborne House, 83-85 Saffron Hill, London EC1N 8RT, England.
www.usborne.com Copyright © 2003, 1997 Usborne Publishing Ltd. The name Usborne and the devices ♀ ⊕ are Trade Marks of
Usborne Publishing Ltd. All rights reserved. No part of this publication may be reproduced, stored in a retrieval system
or transmitted in any form or by any means, electronic, mechanical, photocopying,
recording or otherwise, without the prior permission of the publisher.
Printed in Italy.